Stories Untold This way Better

SHREEYA K

BLUEROSE PUBLISHERS
India | U.K.

Copyright © Shreeya K 2023

All rights reserved by author. No part of this publication may be reproduced, stored in a retrieval system or transmitted in any form or by any means, electronic, mechanical, photocopying, recording or otherwise, without the prior permission of the author. Although every precaution has been taken to verify the accuracy of the information contained herein, the publisher assume no responsibility for any errors or omissions. No liability is assumed for damages that may result from the use of information contained within.

BlueRose Publishers takes no responsibility for any damages, losses, or liabilities that may arise from the use or misuse of the information, products, or services provided in this publication.

For permissions requests or inquiries regarding this publication, please contact:

BLUEROSE PUBLISHERS
www.BlueRoseONE.com
info@bluerosepublishers.com
+91 8882 898 898
+4407342408967

ISBN: 978-93-5741-082-3

Cover design: Tahira
Typesetting: Tanya Raj Upadhyay

First Edition: December 2023

to my aaei, mum, dad and mausi

Table of Contents

Introductions Unchecked 1

Only Box To Fill 3

The Face Of An Upsurge 5

A Heart For A Heart 7

An Attack To the Heart 8

"I Reached" 9

Eight Billion Existences 10

My Pillar 12

Different Question 14

Red String 16

Waited More 18

Swapping Hearts 20

But Still… 22

Sun Worshipping Us 24

The Titanic Poster 26

Fairy Godmother 28

Burning Fire 30

Other Girl 31

Lost 33

Bring Eros To His Knees 35

Polarities of Life 37

The Other Loved 39

Another Step 41

Like Sunshine 43

A Tragic Love Story 45

Wish Upon A Star 47

A Thousand Butterflies	49
July	51
Pretty Lies	53
Mortal Lenses	55
The Story That Matters	57
Destiny Kissing My Face	59
The Skies Full of Infinite Wishes	61
Of Lovely Misinterpretations	63
Heart Precious	65
Flaunt Connections	67
Dearest Dove	69
Outshining Smiles	71
Songs and Pain	73
The Princess's Heart	75
Conditional Love	77
Clouds Of A Dreamer	80
The Sun	82
Red	84
The Girl Who Drowned Everyone	85
Unearthly Trance	88
Big For Two	90
The Marathon	92
Stones and Gold	94

Introductions Unchecked

You sat at the seat with
a book in your hand,
The masked white with polka dots,
Your eyes held an emotion
I could not classify,
I was not a man of words
but of math instead,
I could hold a smile,
But never a conversation,
The same ol' truth instead,
You held a smile as the
teacher introduced me,
and smiled underneath the lies,
At the person,
You thought I would be,
The expectations
you had of me were high,
And as I tried to take
a second look at you,
You turned your face away,
Your eyes, frames and the mask
were all I saw
until your mask lifted,
And a spell was put

you stuttered about your life,

And an introduction

unchecked,

Confident and bold were you,

All the time,

No doubt the teachers,

Had a lot of eyes for you.

-his

Only Box To Fill

You walked in again,

And fear I felt,

But you were entranced,

By the beauty of another

I looked at you again,

Maybe a glimpse would solve

You smiled at me

and I chuckled in return,

Poor you though

I had your heart,

My best friend walked

in with his little blue bag,

And a question deep

planted in my ears,

But the answer never given,

For beauty was not

my only box to fill,

You smiled and chuckled,

All throughout the day,

Everyone stared,

And so did I,

You looked old

but new at the same time,

For those who did not look at

the new kid in class,

On the second day?

-her

The Face Of An Upsurge

The new addition
in your wardrobe,
Dazzled you,
I must say,
But the dirty glares
of your best friend,
Left me unscathed,
You had an opinion,
In the middle of the crowd,
And my hand raised
In your support,
For you were the face
of an upsurge,
I looked at the speech,
But the words flew by,
So I closed my eyes,
And heard your voice,
Everything made sense,
And a killer humour
you did have,
And I raised my hand
in your favour,
For if the face could
not convince me,

The words and confidence,

filled the gaping hole left,

But win you did not,

And I saw you smile,

At the defeat of yourself,

And I giggled inside,

And my friend looked at me,

How out of character I was,

Must I add?

　-his

A Heart For A Heart

Raised my hand,
I impressed a teacher,
For a volunteer option out of school,
And you did the same for another mentor,
With the killer tech skills you had,
A heart for a heart,
What a good friend you were,
And as I looked around for you,
With my best friend's words,
Ringing in my ears on a loop,
For some reason,
I believed in him,
For how could I not,
You had my back like,
A little block of wood on water,
And me on it,
And I found you,
Climbing up the stairs
after you messed up that test,
And I said a hi,
And you said a hello,
And I wish you
A good ol' all the best,
And you worked your brain off,
Oh, I knew.
-her

An Attack To the Heart

The wish for good luck,
Was an attack on my heart,
But you sat in the
bus looking below.
Your eyes met by bag,
And shout you did,
For my safety,
As I wandered about
in the busy street,
"Won't you go with a parent
or in a van?"
you asked,
And I replied,
"No, the parents are busy,
Self is my way, "
"Reach safely,
Text me when you do,"
Was what you said,
With the bus went my heart in it,
And an auto I did ride,
Concern touched my heart,
And I ran home to my phone,
And a text I did send,
But I did nurture it with love,
And loads of it.
-*his*

"I Reached"

A text I did receive

and my bag flung to the ground,

And I grinned at the hot weather,

"I reached",

The simple text read,

It touched my soul,

For in a long time,

After an eternity,

Someone remembered what I said,

And what I reminded,

And I smiled at the camera,

And my pen felt the kindness,

As I scribbled in my notebook,

And my keyboards felt the excitement,

As I typed faster than ever before,

And my, you were the reason,

And as I smiled to myself,

A soul had been

full of sunshine again,

But wouldn't you know,

Because you never liked me,

In the first place.

-her

Eight Billion Existences

I met you again today,
And I glared over your smile,
Exemplary it sure was
your words stole my heart,
In some ways or another,
I boasted how you encrypted
for everyone in the grade,
Knew I was the best tech-person,
And I watched as you,
Smiled and huffed at the comment
as if it was an insult than a praise,
And my best friend stared at me
shaking his head,
Knowing I was,
Fully completely
and happily whipped,
How you whispered
colour into everything
and everywhere,
How the world changed
when you walked in,
And my raps changed
to Ed Sheeran and Harry Styles,
How you dork danced

my way into life again,
Out of the eight billion existences
on the planet,
Yours would be my
absolute favourite.

-his

My Pillar

You made an offer

to support my flair,

Like winds beneath my wings,

I treasured you

like a comfort song,

But I knew

too much gatekeeping,

Would destroy us all,

And you met with me

ignoring all the issues I had,

Dug your way away,

And though the video wasn't abled,

I could still imagine,

Your face

looking at my face,

Peering in for a closer look,

For I wrote my hearts out

and maybe you'd understand,

Of what and how I wrote,

How I was threatened

for feeling,

But you

never judged,

For a new kid,

Who did not know me,
Your were
quite supportive,
And that was that,
You were a pillar,
And my achievements were
the first to reach your ears,
From now and again.

-her

Different Question

You took a screenshot,
And so did I,
And after every achievement,
I stood by,
Remembering the promo text
that you sent,
One of the finest of works that was,
Ideas and hearts were
popping in my brain,
And surely and indefinitely,
Were butterflies
manufactured in my stomach,
You never said
thank you to the group,
But the personal messages
Were your way to make way,
Which made all of us question,
behind your back
why did we not choose her?
You had an arm around writing
and discussed
what you wanted with life,
With me,
Your best friend

forever cautious
of his mouth around me,
Maybe you had
the butterflies for me,
Maybe you didn't,
I made an offer,
And you gladly accepted,
But in a new world,
Maybe a different question
would be the offer,
And you would always say yes.
-his

Red String

You smelled like coffee
on the worst of days,
And like coffee
you cured me,
Of the worst
of my headaches,
Lo! You made me laugh,
Like a little child
In a candy store,
I looked for the chocolates,
But I found
the real gold,
The diamond of chocolates,
Like hugs
from comfort
Like a
little builder,
You build back my ship,
Made of paper,
And set we sail,
And oh we did,
How you
stared and bickered,
And I smiled and replied,

Like a story
written by the stars,
But unsealed by fates,
But I had a
red string on my pink,
I might just
want to see your red string.
-her

Waited More

I looked at you again,
The messages flooded,
And their frequency thriving,
Made me keep guessing
my fate for tomorrow,
Was I just a person
that you texted?
Or the person that
you only texted,
Heart fluttering,
and my arms hugged,
While I waited for
dinner at Vivanta,
I waited more for your text,
A ping and a ding and a buzz,
Kept me more than alive,
What was my
heart's existence for?
If not yours?
And I lived and breathed,
Somedays the same air as you,
And some days,
Even smile,
But now the

texter was the person,

With bigger than life requests,

And as the last text was of you,

Wishing me a good sleep,

And me internally

of your good fortune,

And a good day

of togetherness,

Of adventures ahead.

-his

Swapping Hearts

I saw your face,
Instead of the uniform,
Which merged us together,
You wore jeans and the shirt,
And a bright smile,
With your mask down,
I saw through your eyes
how they lit up
when I walked,
Like a plant
freshly watered,
Glowing in the sun's rays,
Like I was the sun,
In your universe,
You smiled at me again,
And a simple hello was it took,
For me fly in sky of rosy feelings
again,
Praying to all the Gods
and any spirit who might listen,
To let you sit with me
And sit,
Oh you did,
And we talked the way forward,

And all this,
While I wished,
I would feel
that I was good enough,
Good enough for your heart?
And maybe we could swap
each others' hearts
and still keep beating.
-her

But Still...

I saw you dance

within the disco lights,

And you lit up

the bus with your antics,

You smiled,

and I let my heart flutter,

For once again,

It rose to life,

And it thrashed around in its harnesses,

You smiled,

And so did I,

Amidst all this,

Your best friend eyed me,

Afraid I would break you,

And you frowned,

When you saw your

Past come to life,

And you smiled at me

and repeated your story,

Of a girl and a boy

and a ton of unrequited love,

Of a girl and a boy,

And how she moved on,

A girl and a boy,

And how he cussed,
Of a girl and a boy,
And how she destroyed him,
And I laughed,
How you won everything,
And I made a face at the boy,
Hoping he would
burn in hell,
Again and again,
And I saw you,
The glances I gave,
And you nodded
and chided,
'It's all in the past,
And I nodded,
But still' was my answer,
For if I had your heart,
Even for a second,
I would treat it
better than anything,
I ever had.
-his

Sun Worshipping Us

At a ceremony,

I stand

people dancing,

Swaying to the beats,

And drinking out of cups,

And people pushed others,

To dance on the floor,

When I would rather dance with you,

When the skies kiss the earth

Momentarily,

The beginning of the night

to nothing,

But each other's heartbeats,

A weird request to ask of,

But I would dance better with you,

And you would too with me,

Maybe you

dream the same dream

as me,

I hope you do,

Maybe then,

One day,

We could have the same dream,

Become the truth again,

And we would dance again,

Maybe to,

Each other's hearts,

Maybe to the rain,

Maybe to the sun worshipping us,

I wish to know,

What the future holds,

At the same time,

Wish for it to be

with you in it.

-her

The Titanic Poster

I stared at the Titanic poster,

On the tour that we took,

And the fascination your eyes held,

When you smiled at Jack too,

I wanted to be Jack

in that moment,

When you smiled and laughed,

And I wanted to be the one,

At the end of receiving,

The smiles,

The jokes,

And pranks,

And I looked at you,

And you pushed me forward,

"You stand,

with your friend

if you want,"

You said,

But I looked sad,

For I was happy in this spot,

And I was separated,

Because I stood next,

To my bud,

And not next to you,

For who would know,
What would happen to my heart,
If you stood next to me,
For the entirety of 8 hrs,
Maybe I would die,
Maybe I wouldn't,
But the chances of the latter,
Might be higher than others.
-his

Fairy Godmother

Hearts hoped
and brains thought,
Was what they did,
But the story never
ended at a distance,
But where I wanted it to,
I wrote the story,
Then and now,
For now,
You held the ink,
And I held the quill,
Weirdly- heart-breakingly
never seemed to care,
And I did not mean
less about you,
But words stabbed me
better than knives,
And I read of a
thousand confessions,
And more than movies,
I re-enacted them,
But a beating heart
was not an excuse,
For a life-long love ahead,

And I believed in magic
Stronger than other forces,
And I waited,
Till the time
my fairy godmother
showed up.

-her

Burning Fire

I saw you play part
gracefully,
Might I add,
And the captain of this ship
looked nasty as I swayed on,
You sat seats away,
And the teacher pointed you out,
And I grinned
At how you smiled around,
Red were the cheeks,
But it wasn't blush
unless you counted,
The sun making you,
And I gazed at your eyes
and I saw nothing,
And if eyes could write a story,
Ours would be legendary,
Even in the darkest moments,
The eyes you had
burn like fire,
Destroying everything it saw,
And maybe I would laugh at you,
For burning everything at once.
-his

Other Girl

I believed a liar's words,

And I smiled to a trickster in disguise,

A man without feelings

was his heart,

Stone cold and

red was his silhouette,

Hate was his shade,

Love I never did expect,

But a heartbeat for once,

Was an expectation I set,

But when you looked,

At the other girl,

In the middle of life and living,

I thrived off your words,

Support was your glow,

And smiles were your actions,

and I never needed to live,

To tell another tale,

But when I was,

Dragged by the wolves,

Why did the

enchantress enchant you,

That you lost me,

Wholly and completely,

Of a heart that was yours,

And your eyes never meant,

But actions spoke,

Because you never told me,

Anything,

And your heart might be mine,

But your conscience never was,

And I leave with

the baggage I came,

A few lonely hearts,

And higher expectations.

-her

Lost

I lied and I begged

for your heartbeats,

And in front of me stood,

A rejection I despised

the eyes she had weren't,

The ones I used to stare,

But life found a way,

And I lost,

Maybe a gaze

made the difference,

For you and me to know,

Our hearts beat in sync,

But now without a tempo,

It's shattered out of my cage

away for the strangers to read,

The other girl was not my life,

Maybe you were,

I am not sure,

I had a heart,

A true and a happy one,

And its carving is

in your name,

And even if someone dug it,

After a million aeons passing,

Yours would be the name,
Inscribed on it,
Again and again.

-his

Bring Eros To His Knees

Lies spun around me,

Was a world I lived in,

Maybe in a future me,

The comparative degree

of myself,

Would be severed,

But today as I stood

above my body,

I hated the heart,

I gave it to the wolves,

Hating my smile,

And I tore it away,

I hated my speech,

And it never came back,

Throughout my heart being yours,

Yours might be mine,

Maybe today

maybe tomorrow

maybe forever

maybe never?

But I was a person

and people forever replaceable

maybe I would too be,

Lost in your heart,

Searching for your most,
While she gets it all,
You and your smile,
And that cunning charm,
That could bring Eros,
To his knees.
-her

Polarities of Life

Maybe I cut you deep,

Maybe I destroyed a true heart,

Maybe my sins and lies,

My past and stupidity

finally caught up,

And forever would be a promise,

Maybe none of us could keep,

And a funny story,

Now turns to thriller,

As you anticipate my move,

And calculate what yours would be,

Hearts broken,

Eyes spilt,

Over the year,

We did it all,

Smiled and cried,

Laughed and shouted,

Screamed and joked,

Amongst the polarities of life,

I met you,

A juxtaposition personified,

And now you walk farther away,

The other girl,

Oh may I condemn her,

My heart was never hers,
And I swear that in the name,
Of you,
Forever and never.

-his

The Other Loved

I might see you after
the harsh hot suns,
And so my heart thumped,
For what the summer witnessed
only summer knew,
Neither I wished nor prayed,
For a glance from you,
For I just saw you briefly,
As I walked to my
best friend throne,
And re-thinking our dynamic,
Were we just strangers I thought?
Just looking and peering
into each other's lives
as we rambled on,
Without our thoughts and feelings
stabbing us in the back,
How would I be sure
that you would not turn out
like the same old love
That harboured my heart a while ago,
Ages later
maybe our souls might
know each other

maybe we would be spectacular?
Maybe musical,
Even legendary perhaps
or maybe just strangers
harbouring and peering into,
Each other's lives
once in a while
And wishing it was us,
That the other loved.
-her

Another Step

Time passes
as it usually does
But the heart
never agrees,
How you lost the game
for when did I stand a chance
against the
centrepiece herself?
The games played were many,
Let's see who
stays away longer
or the let me ghost you,
They didn't interest you
so I did what I did most
flatter,
So when the days reached
to a back breaking toil,
Honey laced
words sent to you,
And the replies came,
Divided was the attention given,
But for a person with ADHD
you gave your best,
Times were wasted

and skills shown off,
as if I were a peacock trying to
ruffle my feathers to look bigger,
And a certain peahen came,
Giving the best gift of all,
To make another step
for us to climb.

-his

Like Sunshine

You felt like sunshine,
Maybe that is why it pained,
But your eyes begged,
and I never gave in,
And my best friend
sighed of my fate again,
He knew what would happen,
As if his predictions
happened every year,
But the heart was there
in that mortal carcass
somewhere,
The week went by,
And the suns rose and fell,
And your hints, if I took,
Were many to count,
And my heart fell apart,
Between you and me,
If love was falling,
Then I didn't fall to my death,
You never killed me,
And you never shall,
Light be shown,
My heart would

forever be yours,
Like it always was,
There was never a time,
That it wasn't yours
And forgiveness is a
virtue earned,
For everything you did,
Because,
This time,
I wasn't the sun,
You were,
And my eco-systems needed,
You in the end
for survival and life.
-her

A Tragic Love Story

Life never fair
but always forgiving,
And I stood dejected
like a character at the end
of a tragic love story,
With a bouquet in my hands
and tears in my eyes,
Somehow,
I was the tragic hero
who turned you
into the tragic damsel,
Maybe I clouded your thoughts,
And if I could wish for it,
Then surely I would,
How I dreamt
that you could see,
How funny you could be,
With my simple LMFAO,
How hard I laughed
at the end of the days,
Dejected you were,
At the end of the gruelling week,
Your terms shifted,
As I confessed,

Of past love,
You sweetly poisoned
 the mind,
And I gladly drank,
And at the end of the day,
It wasn't poison,
But ambrosia instead.

-his

Wish Upon A Star

Across the students sitting,

Eyes of your stuck out

From a sea of thousand seas,

I remembered

the one that I forgave,

You laughed and smiled

and I noticed all of it,

The chuckles after

a breathless laughter,

Knowing smirks after

an inside joke,

Trying smiles of courage,

how you never gave up,

Loud laughter,

Which made my

Heart fill with joy,

Like it overflowed,

Till it could no more

how you tried so much,

But in silence

like effortlessly you won,

Graceful as the

ballerina who danced,

Taking the

limelight of my heart,
how could I say?
That the new kid
was the Romeo,
When you were the Orpheus,
To my Eurydice,
Maybe in other universes,
Maybe you might
Wish upon a star,
But now as the clock strikes
11:11, I wished
for you to be.
-her

A Thousand Butterflies

Out of all the dreams I dreamt,

The dreams of you

would be the highest,

Dancing in the spotlight,

Or just in the corner,

Like we knew the secret

and we both held the keys,

To a world,

Both of us swore by,

The excitement of

a thousand butterflies,

Your heart

and my words,

Or maybe the other way around,

Maybe messages could never say,

Or maybe I was ignorant,

Incoherent and never hopeful

about the world we lived in,

The truths flew in

that the new kid

was your favourite,

And I believed it,

For the way you sung,

In your minstrel voice,

Showed all that
I needed to know,
But as they say,
You did not fall from
the pedestal,
That you made for yourself,
because you flew
for the old kid,
Time flew by
and I was the original
now.
-his

July

I could let July be July,
Full of showers,
And pakode and chais ahead,
But a day was all it took
For it to be special,
Full of rains that year was,
And you saw
how my eyes crackled,
As the thunder did outside,
Saying,
Your are the moment, dear,
And I froze in the weather
Of how you smiled at me,
Cheeks tilted upwards,
Was your statue to be made
while other characters smirked
you laughed your hearts out,
Was it a fact known,
that ladies dug funny guys
then you portrayed
 it to perfection,
With all my hopes and wishes,
I had for being a teenager,
Except life and career,

Mind and body,
I wished that,
You were the person,
Who you were to be,
And not the actor
made out in,
The middle of a fight.

-her

Pretty Lies

The oceans kissed the stars today,
And I heard a pretty lie
Of how your heart yearned for me,
Over the summer times,
Friends, fights and yearnings for love,
Who would I be in this equation?
I doubt,
Never the constant in life,
Always the variable,
Lost in the echo of life,
Like a beat of a heart,
Left alone,
But the rains it did happen
and your heart I did see,
If what you wrote was true
then heavens help,
Your heart might be real,
The paper still in my bag,
For hard to let it go,
After a day of confrontation,
I let it go,
For if you had a voice,
You sure shouted,
And if I had a voice,

I would whisper happily,
What a great pair we made.

-his

Mortal Lenses

Confessions laid out

the fanfare crazy

but missing out,

The hottest gala of yours,

Never my regret,

How the mortal lenses,

Failed to capture,

Of how fulfilling,

Your soul was,

Like a ray of sunshine,

On an early sunny day,

If the teams were made

I would pick you,

Because the truth clear,

New was out with the old,

Never the new kid,

You were now,

And the old kid you became,

For the faculty knew your name

and the students your rumours,

Amongst broken lies

and toe-tipped,

The lines of black and white,

Sadness and pains,

With a single wand,
If I could,
I would wish for the world
to make you happy,
because the world?
Could use people like you.
-her

The Story That Matters

Your life planned out,
Dreams, hopes and colleges alike,
And I stood in the crowd,
Never knowing what to do,
And the workshops,
From the seniors said it all,
What I want
And need,
My questions laid out,
The answers given,
The subject, colleges and life alike,
And I dreamt of a time,
When I knew you,
Without knowing you,
Questions asked,
And you showered me
With love,
What a day it was,
You, me and the
Hopes of it all,
At the end,
That the story
does that matter?
And your support,

I always had,

For the end always had,

Something special,

Forever and always.

-his

Destiny Kissing My Face

Happily I could declare
that your soul allured me,
But the flattery you gave
unparalleled by any and all,
For the words you spoke,
And the dreams
that you weaved,
Hearts and hands laid out,
A picnic basket by our side
in a mind of one,
There was place for two
for the both of us,
Against time and space,
Two rogue humans,
Fighting cosmic forces,
For you had a heart,
And I had one too,
What connected them
was the story untold,
At the end,
When the ball was
 in your court,
And you had to pass
the ball was dribbled,

And passed right on my face,
Like destiny kissing me.

-her

The Skies Full of Infinite Wishes

Hi's and hello's were spread,

But decency ran low,

Rumours spread

faster than love,

And angry my love,

You ravaged houses and palaces

for how dreadful lives can be,

And a letter sent to me

under your name,

And the proclamations many,

Your hearts full of love

and I proclaimed my love,

The glow of your eyes,

Held the power of suns,

Thousands blaring,

Into the face of the earth,

Hugging and smiling

As I stood by,

Strong you were,

Brighter you shined,

Higher you flew,

And maybe my declaration,

Freed you

and with your dreams,

In my eyes,
Wishing you all the best,
We both flew
into the skies
full of infinite wishes.
-his

Of Lovely Misinterpretations

From blocked to loved,

The transition swift,

And the hanging threads

of lovely misinterpretations

left my friends unheard,

True or not,

Floated the word,

None of us confirming

or denying,

But the stars said

something else,

And the moon

nodded too,

For our words

never contradicted,

Each other's tongues,

Pure symphony was

the organ's name,

And we played it wonderfully,

and you wanted to whisper,

The love in

trees and little flowers,

But the roar of our proclamation,

Was heard over

The guzzling seas,
The roaring thunder and
the powerful storms,
And strong we were,
But never to fight the world,
And we lived in peace
Again till the time,
Would be a boring end
to this fairy tale,
Yet the twists were here
To be and live and thrive,
And our conversations
touched time and space,
Like never before,
And reality ran away
hoping to catch us in 4k,
But doubtfully never did,
For we ran sprints and marathons,
And this time
we had two,
And we could win
if you would be there.
-her

Heart Precious

Interpretations indeed left out,
But words and actions indeed showed,
For your heart could never ever beat for me,
For fear I did,
Of your wrath and rage,
And love I never did,
For if I were the peasant,
You ruled the world,
And no matter the reconciliations had,
I would always miss out,
And your heart precious
than liquid gold,
And powerful were the words of the smith,
And the joy you gave me was plenty,
But I had your heart once,
And it lay shattered
amongst the glass pieces,
Forgiveness was your conduct
and destruction was the way of my life,
Who knew the old kid would ever
Destroy the oldest so much,
That the paper would bleed from the ink,
And the story ended,

When I put a full stop,

At the end,

When you wanted to put a semicolon.

-his

Flaunt Connections

Burned the flesh that made you
who you were,
For the friendship that
the whole world applauded
and cry my eyes I did,
Under the stars every night
forgiveness a conduct of yours
smile boy, smile boy,
And flaunt everyone did
that their connections
started with you
hate everyone I did,
Back and forth
back and forth
back and forth,
Went the boat of our lives
I took you in
the deep blue ocean,
With the trust in your eyes
your body followed
cross the sea we did
but leave you in the middle?
For the pain I created in your heart,
For the break in

your chemical balance,
Did the body hurt
when your mind knew,
That mind didn't run
after you anymore?
Afraid I would hurt again,
I run away
again
and again.
-her

Dearest Dove

When your tears
touched hands,
And my screams
of pain were unheard of
shout
scream
cry
was what you did at me
at you
dearest dove,
Don't you fight
with yourself,
It burns your existence
into ashes of a former embrace,
Disintegrating into unknown
were you doing something new?
Let the rains cry
over the lands,
making them fertile
and bounty
from everything to nothing,
I saw it all
in a month
how fast did times change,

The noose fastly tied to you
and never a word uttered,
Dearest dove don't you
cry to yourself,
For a shoulder stands here
to be a hanging thread
for tears leak acid
and burn the deepest
holes in people,
Not love could ever
fill that acid hole
let the tears flow,
But not the ones of rage
for they burn
the world around you
and me in it.
-his

Outshining Smiles

When the days when your smile
outshined the street lamps,
When the sun took
the wrong turns
 to end up in the scary nooks,
And the banging inside the cage
that which you calls mind,
Shouts and wreaks havoc
in the corner of
every visceral organ,
and the best traveller in
 the land travel across
the oceans,
To meet every creature
and structure and home
and palace,
But never the thing
That wrote your worth,
The whispers amongst the crowd,
Of the gait and walk and
the talks he talked,
The armour you wore

or the swords you hold,

When the clan of your blood

spoke of heights to conquer.

-her

Songs and Pain

The minstrels sung of
love and pain
and the greatest sagas,
But the fear of not a
love to be conquered
weighed less,
Than the land I had to call
own,
And the fear I felt weighed you
lower and lower into the grave dug,
A question to inherit was
the herculean task to comprehend,
For the land left by your brother
in your name
to be won and razed
when the day changes to night,
And the ghostly face
of the moon appears,
The next day the
sun revisits his kingdom,
After fighting with death himself,
To give light and life
to all his subject,
And the stars keep shining

whether he looks at it
or changes his mind,
If the head did
turn upwards,
Then the gods
shall bless you,
And rise you shall.
-his

The Princess's Heart

A story of a girl who trusted easy
caution and pain lace
a story such as ours,
Sharp metal cut
her heart out of the viscera,
Divided into pieces was
the metal he held,
The lineal crest on
his chest saved his face,
Alas! Assassins never
make good lovers,
Hearts stolen,
And kingdoms
looted,
In the empty streets,
What else was left to steal?
After he ransacked
the pride, love, respect
and power her crown held?
Bloody was the shroud
that he laid her in,
The future crown never receiving
the ceremonial goodbye deserved,
In the godly lights,

The moons sighed,
And the stars wept,
For the grand declarations
And the love bore by them,
Results in the most brutal murders,
The love might be hoax,
Otherwise the dots
Didn't line up,
And the princess lay there,
Floating away from
Her name, kingdom and power,
And Osiris welcomed me with open arms,
For the celestials knew,
That the crown
Loved and trusted
Too deep
And too easy,
And a heart unguarded
Was a heart waiting to be attacked.
-her

Conditional Love

I wonder about the sadder days
when the wheels of your mind
were only mine,
Of the more blue days when
you could never care less about
others' problems,
And the days when I just hoped
that the sun would not shine
and rain would start to pour
just so you could vibe with
me in the gloomy weather.
Telephone lines cut,
and my wifi plugged in,
And my
earphones did not help,
And I tried to cut
out the drowning and the
sinking I felt,
But I could not be more
wrong about when you
gave out your hand,
And I laughed saying I
belonged to the seas.
But now I drown, and rain

poured down on
my sad, gloomy self,
When I ask for the golden
rays I am given none,
For how does the sun not
distinguish between conditional love,
And your mind and the
pretty hand were missed
by me far more than presumed.
I tried to cry and shout
for help,
Oh my dear,
I try,
But my head is underwater
for so long that my skin
wrinkles,
I try to touch
the sun again and
hear your lovely voice again,
Oh my love,
I do try,
But the water does not
let its possession leave.
A long time ago,
when I was
your favourite,

and you were my lifeline,

Along the lines of love

and promises of infinity,

You left my hand,

And I let you go,

But now I drown,

And I wonder of the days

when your hand was

 always out-stretched,

What if now I ask

Is it still for me?

Would you still believe me

if I gave you the reason of love,

Would the pain subside in

our hearts better than

distance drove us apart

in each others' hearts,

At the end of every letter and song

and poem I wrote of love,

I missed your heart and

hand and mind,

Would you believe me and

tell me my love is not

conditional like you did all those months ago?

-his

Clouds Of A Dreamer

The book closes on
the mahogany kitchen table,
But the half written
story's spoilers made known,
All my eyes turning
to red after weeping,
The book unfinished is
the plot where I lost hope,
And the side characters bow
and bang their chests over,
The untimely despair
bestowed upon them.
The dried crimson shade
paint the floorboards,
The white tiles shine
upon the glorious sun,
When the sharpest of
knives glitter around,
The drops of pain
stretched across the heads,
The pain etched in
the mortal body and
the red stain dyed,
With the period put at

the last page and
the story finished.
The last day rolled in
after the million
pages turned,
And the last skywatcher
could see the clouds
named after the dreamer,
But the darkest clouds
covered the starry skies
showing the
colours of the dreamer,
And the children
left bored
of the villagers'
tales of boring gods.
-her

The Sun

The sun always stayed.
Like a constant.
Never speeding away,
When things got hard.
When the clouds
fought and cried.
He rooted for them.
Gave them space.
And let them be.
Heartless as it sounds,
The sun could
Not a person.
And it never would be,
Because it had been there,
Forever and always.
When the day was good,
When the night was bad,
How I wish you
could be the sun,
Like a constant,
Never leaving my story,
Alas, the universe
gave privileges to the sun,
Like the warmth in his veins.
The golden glow could heal all.

How he healed
every creature around him,
Life giving and healing.
How noir was it of you?
To destroy everything
You touched.
If medusa had a story,
You have none.
If the sun met you.
He would never hurt or
pain the souls you saved.
Like a forbearing cover,
The pain he would absorb.
Like the king of the ecosystem,
A place you could never have,
To be the sun.
How wonderful must it be?
To have everyone love you?
To have the power?
To have the care and nature?
To heal all around you?
But you cannot ask for that,
Even if you're his daughter,
You cannot be the sun to me.
You could never be,
For he stands on a pedestal,
You can never reach.
-his

Red

Red were the
hearts that broke,
Red was the
blood that stained your hands,
Red was the
shade of a first love's truth,
Red was the
shade I cried every night,
Red was the
tint of his first meeting cheeks,
Red was his
colour of love,
Red were the
eyes when we left,
Red was the
bench where we first met.

-her

The Girl Who Drowned Everyone

When the clear surface touches
the farthest corners of the earth,
Apollo routinely
drove his chariot around earth,
All the while,
Poseidon connived
against a brother.
Dark skies of Zeus's rage
chased away the
ichor in the skies,
In search for the
oceanic treasures
you left your father's legacy.
Surfing and kissing
in the panoramic views,
Made sense in
the sunshine's kiss,
And the last lap given by
lady luck to run away,
Echoes from the past
and the fast paced reminders passing by,
The plot burnt high
and low in waves of ravage,
Alas the sun complains

for his child.
The waves rode high
and razed the world on touch,
Poseidon rolled away
the childish commands away,
The marathon for
the sands commenced.
Your friends ran
for their lives,
feet trailing back,
Alas! they could only run
after a kiss from death.
The day you stood,
Your father and
your aunt met together,
How does your heart
not break?
From the pain and the guilt
of being the one who
drowned everyone.
Under you went and
the lord of the sea ran above you,
Till oxygen left the body,
The body floated on the surface.
For once light
bowed to death,

for once,

Your soul chirpy and happy,

Left to the forever

loop of never ending darkness.

-his

Unearthly Trance

Mom, I don't wanna go
crash, boom and thud
the crashes and
the gritty cobblestones,
All the stars that the red
in my eyes could never see,
The deadly deaths
of the one who could
ever take my heart
around me.
Mom, I don't wanna go
burn, crackle and sizzle
the loud siren horns and
the screeches of a new war,
With the soul that saved me,
Red marks burning
into the orange flesh,
The flesh slowly
turns to animal skin.
Mom, I don't wanna go,
The last plunge taken
blub-glub and gasps
of air later
The blue of the entirety

turns to the known obsidian,
Cry, shout, scream and pant
and the glow of an
unearthly trance takes me under.
-her

Big For Two

The white mask and
polka dot hidden face,
I reminisced it all
the tiny glances snuck across,
The turn-away gazes
as if my eyes
belonged as the
disputed property,
Longing through
the glasses fogged up
Your eyes's lenses
as they breathed life
into your chocolate orbs,
Once my favourite
shade to see around
I knew it all around the world,
As if the sun revolved around you
and your moves
were all I remembered,
Each detail you mentioned,
Dog breed you befriend
colour of your future home
aesthetic it would have
your future dreams

and your lyrics shared,
Tattooed on my heart strings
 were the things about you,
That even erosion
could not resolve to erase
the pain you suffer
I feel it too,
Know a heart is big for two
And once a home is made,
It's harder to destroy.
-his

The Marathon

I never learnt to swim
for my shoulder was
near your neck
life support I trusted
with my soul,
Now lay in puddles of blood,
I pay the price of falling
into the water with you
never knowing
how fast
it would
become hot,
And my heart I gave,
You took it
and took care of it
Along the trail
one heart lost
and a life you gained,
A sister forged
by my blood,
Reminding how her brother
lost a love in
the ball drop at midnight,
Destroyed a palace

I built overnight of memories
Like it stood on sand,
Oh, when would you have,
I would have stood
out like a wine stain
Forbidden
and unlikable
and bitter,
The keys to your
house joined to my heart,
Left my boots out in the rain
and you run
after umbrella holders
to find the legs that fit
in boots, I ran after you,
And silver wouldn't be enough
to repel the hearts
that pained,
No matter how
far time travels,
It comes back to
a time where
the marathon we ran together
not after one.
-her

Stones and Gold

I wear your boots
draining the water
to climb the stage
with your name on it,
To be the legendary Romeo
to recite Shakespeare
and a piece written by hand,
I told a story of a car,
And you smiled
when you checked,
When I added
a reference to us,
But the look of glee ran away
As fast it came
dethroned by
something else,
The face turned
 to a question,
With the sign and a pen
I make a scratch
on the paper,
The one I held near my heart
that kept me alive,
I breath in the stories

you weaved,
I added the glitter,
And the story left
 behind was your heart,
The last words exchanged
 resulted to a painful
exchange of those orbs,
Chocolate my favourite,
And your brother eyes me
uncertainty
guilt,
I was no diamond
No miner could mine
a stone lying on the road.
How could a stone sit
with the gold rays of the sun?
Find a diamond
It would shine like you
never dimming,
The most radiant of all.
But a diamond is cut now
Wouldn't be reversed.
-him

www.ingramcontent.com/pod-product-compliance
Lightning Source LLC
LaVergne TN
LVHW041621070526
838199LV00052B/3203